Contents

Published in Great Britain by
World International Publishing Limited,
P.O. Box 111, Great Ducie Street, Manchester M60 3BL.
Printed in Great Britain.
SBN 7235 6747 6.

The FELLOWSHIP of QUAN

The dark tunnel resonated with a wheezing, groaning sound. A translucent shape solidified into the Tardis. The door opened, and the Doctor stepped out.

Peri asked, as she followed him out, "Where are we?"

The Doctor gave a haughty sniff. "Appears to be a tunnel!" he said.

"You said Tuven III was uninhabited, but this tunnel looks manmade!"

The Doctor replied in exasperation to her seemingly rhetorical question. "I don't know, it isn't every day that I come to this planet!"

Peri clicked her tongue, looking at the rough-hewn walls of the cylindrical passage.

"Sorry about the bumpy landing," the Doctor added in a more conciliatory tone. "The lateral balance off-set needs a cleaning."

The tunnel had a ghostly luminescence, caused by the fluorescent rocks. "Aren't you going to do the repairs?" Peri's voice echoed down the dank tunnel.

The Doctor began casually walking down the passage. "I'll let the Tardis' automatic systems sort it out."

The tunnel ended in an arched portal, and they passed through it into a large round room, still with bare rock walls like the tunnel, but better lit.

The Doctor examined a cylindrical control column, with flickering coloured lights on its surface, standing on a raised dais in the centre of the room. "I've found the control panel, Peri," he said, the reflected lights dancing on his face. He passed a hand over one panel light, and the room was flooded with light.

Peri paced around the room, while the Doctor fed his insatiable curiosity. Peri was speechless when she saw camouflaged hatches open around the wall and a row of gun nozzles protruded. "Doctor, get down!" she cried in time and they both dropped to the ground. The nozzles spouted a torrent of bullets, the staccato roar deafening them, bullets ricochetting and whizzing over their heads. Finally the furious rapid fire ceased, and the nozzles retracted. Peri rose and rushed to the motionless Doctor. "Doctor!" He opened his eyes and beamed. "That wasn't funny, especially as I can guess who caused that to happen! Someone poking around!"

"An accident, an unfortunate blunder..." the Doctor tailed off. "You're right. By accident I operated the computer's defence system." The Doctor glanced at the computer terminal, frowning deeply. "Odd computer that, it insists that the tunnel network is submerged."

"That means we could just be in an air pocket!" said Peri in alarm.

"Let's get to the Tardis," said the Doctor.

Three black robed and cowled figures watched them on a monitor screen embedded in a large rock. It began to replay the Tardis' materialisation. "This endangers the Fellowship of Quan," said one named Svan.

Passon voiced his own fears. "He could harm the faith, Sentinel."

The Sentinel of Quan nodded solemnly, face hidden by the hood. "The risk is grave," he said, as the recording showed the Doctor at the control console before the hail of bullets was released. "And yet he has some knowledge of the old machines. Prevent their escape, whilst I consider what to do with him."

Peri and the Doctor had almost reached the Tardis when the ground began to shake, vibrations running through the tunnel, reverberating with a dull thundering. Suddenly the tunnel overhead collapsed. Heavy rocks narrowly missed them, but most of the debris consisted of glittering sand grains, which cascaded down upon them. The surging sands finally settled, and Peri and the Doctor stumbled to their feet,

covered in fluorescent particles.

The Doctor was furious. "The computer was right, we are submerged under two miles of sand!"

Peri softly said, "Oh, no," and the Doctor followed her gaze to the buried Tardis. Only the light atop the police box showed, "I guess we dig," said Peri.

The Doctor knelt before the Tardis, examining the sand grains. "Look, Peri!" he coaxed.

"Doctor, when you've seen one sand grain, you've seen 'em all!"

"Indeed!" retorted the Doctor. "For your information, this is not natural sand, the grains are too angular. Perhaps the computer can tell us why." He bounded off towards the control room.

"Good, Passon," said the Sentinel in satisfaction. The monitor showed the buried Tardis. The Sentinel added ruefully, "If only you could revive Quan, who lies in perpetual sleep."

"Shall we capture them now?" asked Svan.

"Yes," hissed the Sentinel. "Alive!"

The Doctor studied the computer console. "Just as I thought, Peri! Those grains were angular because they were machined! The entire planet surface was machined."

"But is that possible?" asked Peri.

The Doctor continued. "Machined by an army of robots for centuries!"

Peri hissed, "Doctor!"

"What?"

"We've got company!"

He looked up from the console; they were surrounded by robed figures. "Greetings," he began uncertainly, "we'd love to chat but..."

The robed wraiths grabbed them and, after a lengthy journey through the tunnel matrix, they were thrown into the Sentinel's chamber.

Svan, Passon and the Sentinel stood before the monitor screen.

"I don't like your tailor's choice of colours!" quipped the Doctor.

"Silence before the Sentinel!"

the Doctor produced machine pistols.

"Very persuasive," said the Doctor wryly.

Later he stood before an ornate door set into the wall of a room adjoining the Sentinel's chamber. They had been told to try and decipher an inscription. The Doctor wrote notes on a pad with a pencil, both supplied by Peri. The cowled Sentinel watched from a dark corner. "Here lies Quan," said the Doctor aloud. "Whoever would wish to free him does so at his own cost, for Quan will kill to protect his brethren."

"Thank you, Doctor," said the Sentinel, in a gloating tone. "That is all I wished to know. Really your expertise with machines was not what I required, your ability to

bellowed Svan.

"Sentinel?" Peri queried.

"The Sentinel, supreme protector of the faith, he who knows all," ranted Passon.

"Why do you bring us here?" asked the Doctor bluntly.

"Your knowledge is required," responded Passon.

"A paradox! The Sentinel knows all, but needs me!"

"Who are you people?" asked Peri.

The Doctor answered for her. "I'll tell you," he said. "The computer informed me that they are the survivors of the mineral exploitation years. They drained their own planet of minerals using robots. They destroyed their planet's biosphere with widespread mining, residing here underground like rats now because their planet has become a shifting sea of sand. Dead."

"But Quan will save us!" shouted Svan.

"We are his followers," said Passon.

"It is written that he is our creation, and salvation," said the Sentinel, in a voice which was vaguely familiar to the Doctor. "He will wake to save us one day."

"So you need me to wake Quan, using machinery you don't understand how to use? I'll bet this Quan is in suspended animation."

"It is true that your help is needed," said the Sentinel sadly. "But if you do not co-operate, you will be shot."

At his unspoken command, the two 'brothers' guarding Peri and decipher such inscriptions was all I needed.''

The Doctor scrutinised the Sentinel. ''That voice is masked by something, a voice synthesizer!'' he said, and rushed forward, pulling the hood back. Peri sucked her breath in. The dark, brushed-back hair and the pointed beard were unmistakable, it was the Master!

''What's your part in all this?'' demanded the Doctor.

The Master smiled sourly. ''Quan is a robot, designed to protect his fellow robots who mined this planet, his 'brethren'.''

The Doctor pointed to a disc strapped to the Master's throat. ''And that?''

''A simple trick to copy the original Sentinel's voice. He had an unfortunate accident with my Tissue Compression Eliminator. You can imagine.''

''How did you draw us here?'' asked Peri.

''I used one of the machines created by the ancestors of these morons. It causes a localised spacial vortex. Risky, but effective. It pulled your Tardis here.''

They were interrupted by the arrival of Svan and Passon. The Master hurriedly pulled his cowl up, clutching the disc voice synthesizer to his throat. ''It is done! Open the hatch, Svan!'' cried the Master. Together with Passon, Svan pulled the thick metal door open.

''No, you fools, this is not your Sentinel!''

Guards covered the Doctor and Peri. The instant the hatch opened, the green liquid used for suspension spilled out all over the floor. Illuminated by its own strange iridescence, a squat robot, shorter than a man, stood within. It had a rounded flattened face, with small piggish facial features. Its body was ridged, with heavy overlapping metal plates. Quan leapt to the floor before the astonished watchers.

The Master, clutching the disc to his throat, said, ''I am the one who caused your awakening.''

Quan tried to speak, but only the green suspension fluid spilled from its mouth. Then it said, in a high, piggish voice, ''Where are my brothers?''

''We are your brothers,'' interceded Svan encouragingly.

"Humans? Where are my robot brethren?"

"They are gone, my friend," cooed the Master. "Only you remain, with me as your guide in this time, which is new to you."

"What do you ask in return?"

The Master made a note of its quick response time; that could be dangerous. "I offer a symbiotic relationship, mutually profitable to us both. I will use you to conquer, to exploit others."

"How will this benefit me?"

"A purpose, a Master—what else could a machine want?" The Master was growing impatient.

The Doctor interceded. "You have no reason to follow an off-worlder. Why not serve the creators of the robots you once protected?"

The Master whirled round, "Silence him!"

"No," bellowed Svan. "Let him speak. Who are you?"

"I am the Doctor. I am of this man's race, the Time Lords."

Svan spluttered, "Liar! This is the Sentinel, our most respected citizen, he who watches over his people."

"Whoever that was, he's dead. The Master killed him and uses a machine to copy his voice. Just as his face is cloaked, so is his voice."

Quan ruminated on the Doctor's words. "You speak the truth. With infra-red vision I can see the heat trace of the device. I will never trust an off-worlder. I will do as you suggest, Doctor, serve my people."

The furious 'brothers' closed in on the Master.

"Time to leave," hissed the Doctor. He and Peri soon cleared the sand from the Tardis.

"Shouldn't we help him, Doctor?" asked Peri.

"You know better than most how ruthless he is. On this occasion he can reap what he sowed," said the Doctor adamantly.

The Master looked from side to side as the menacing crowd walled him in. A hand shot forth, pulling back his hood, revealing his true identity. "No, please," he said, discarding the voice synthesizer. "Please, Doctor!" he cried. But the echoing call fell on deaf ears; the Tardis had gone.

TIME WAKE

"Why here, Doctor?" Peri asked for the third time, as she glanced at the deserted road ahead, not a soul in sight. She and the Doctor were walking along the wet pavement of an early morning London street.

The Doctor, seemingly oblivious to Peri, held a small black box before him, and was watching a meter intently. The box made a plaintive bleeping sound. "Because, Peri," he finally answered, "the time anomaly is very close."

Peri paused, considering this, then asked, "What is a 'time anomaly'?"

"It's a phenomenon which shouldn't be there," he replied tersely. "Using the Tardis tracking equipment I was able to pinpoint it to this area, in the special temporal dimensional and geographical sense, of course."

"Of course," echoed Peri. She was all too familiar with the Doctor's incorrigible curiosity, but this time it was different, she thought: the Doctor seemed worried by what he called the Time Wake. "Is there any danger?" she asked.

"It seems as if someone is using a very primitive, unstable time vessel."

"Sounds like the Tardis," Peri muttered.

"Whoever the operator is, he could cause a major time slip," continued the Doctor. "You see, his primitive craft has left a Wake in the space-time vortex, rather like the wake left behind by a ship at sea. The Wake extends between the present day..."

"January, 1986," Peri interjected.

"Yes, and 1720," added the Doctor curtly.

The bleeping from the Doctor's machine increased in pitch. "We must be close!" he said excitedly. The Doctor stopped, sweeping the box in a wide circle around him, then swivelled back sharply: the bleeping was loudest in the road's direction.

The Doctor walked with the box at arm's length, Peri behind him, until they reached the middle of the road. The bleeping reached its highest pitch as the Doctor lowered the box over a man-hole cover leading down to the sewers. He gave an apologetic smile, and Peri nodded her head in silence, resigned at what was to follow. In restrained silence, hands on hips, she watched the Doctor lift free the sewer cover; she could smell the sewer stench rising already. The Doctor gave his lucky charm, the lapel cat, a little pat before disappearing into the black depths. His voice floated up with the smell. "Coming or not, Peri?" he said. Peri looked down the hole, shrugged her shoulders, and gingerly climbed down the ladder.

She and the Doctor stood on a ledge running along the sewer wall. At first she thought the circle of light on the opposite wall was from the Doctor's pen torch.

The Doctor said, "Look! That wall has an iridescence of its own."

"But how?" Peri asked, looking at the eerie light.

"Must be the end of the Time Wake! Come on!" The Doctor jumped athletically from the raised side of the sewer floor they had been standing on to the other on the opposite wall. Peri was more hesitant; she had no desire to fall into the sewer stream between herself and the Doctor. She leapt over the metre and a half gap, clinging to the damp brick wall for safety. The bright glowing patch was near to them, and they walked along to it.

"If we don't catch this buffoon, he could cause havoc!" warned the Doctor.

Peri's voice betrayed the concern she felt. "Shouldn't we go in the Tardis?" she asked.

"No time, Peri! The trail will be gone by the time we reach the

Tardis. The Time Wake will heal itself in a few hours. Now, hold my hand!" The Doctor and Peri leapt at the brick wall, and Peri shrieked in alarm, expecting to hit solid stone. Instead, she and the Doctor entered a short luminescent tunnel, through which they floated to another glowing point. They landed feet first on firm ground.

The Doctor looked around. They were in a cellar, with a glowing circle of light on the wall behind them, like the one in the sewer. The other end of the Time Wake. "Here we are, Peri, 1720, eighteenth century London." The Doctor, using his pen torch, surveyed the cellar.

Peri watched the Time Wake mournfully. Was it contracting? The air was cool around them, and dimly Peri could see barrels of ale. "What is this place?"

"The cellar of an inn. That time machine has to be near. It's probably rather large and heavy. Difficult to move it elsewhere." They searched the cellar high and low, but could not find the machine.

"Maybe it's got a chameleon circuit like the Tardis," Peri suggested, adding ruefully, "one that works."

The Doctor was obviously hurt. "For your information," he lectured, "only the more advanced species in the Universe have such technology. Judging by our friend's clumsy mode of transport, he does not!"

Peri smiled to herself at the Doctor's indignant reply, then noticed something sticking out of the cellar wall. She looked closely at the long ridge. It was a door. "Doctor!" she called. "Come and see."

The Doctor looked. "A secret passage! Well done, Peri! Now you stay here..."

"Are you kidding? I'm not staying in this creepy place."

The Doctor flashed a conciliatory smile, and they both opened the secret door. They entered a narrow passage. The torch showed a door at the end of it, which they opened. As they stepped into the room, all thoughts of furtive entry and keeping out of sight were forgotten as they were confronted by a bizarre spectacle. The long room contained rows of large glass tubes, glowing from within, each filled with a swirling mist which failed to hide the occupants. The two time travellers instantly recognised the people.

At last the Doctor spoke. "British Prime Ministers! Extraordinary!"

"It's weird, like someone collected them, the way you might collect butterflies."

"Every Prime Minister is here," confirmed the Doctor, "from Walpole to Pitt the Younger, to

Disraeli and Gladstone, Lloyd George, Churchill, Wilson and Thatcher."

"But how can they all be here?" queried Peri. "We know that none were kidnapped."

"Do we?" snapped the Doctor. "You're probably right. They must be android replacements, facsimiles of the real persons, kept in suspended animation."

"But why? Why stop at Mrs Thatcher?"

"Whoever made the Time Wake came from 1986, and Mrs Thatcher was PM at that time," said the Doctor. "Our traveller must have had historical data up to that time. No doubt gained in 1986."

"So he could make a copy of every British Prime Minister up until 1986? It's crazy!"

Unseen, a figure in a long black cloak stepped into the secret passage and closed the door.

The Doctor heard the door close, and rushed to it. It was locked. "He must have seen us and realised we knew too much!" the Doctor shouted.

"What do you mean?" Peri was answered by the hum of machinery, and they watched in horror as each glass tube slid into the ceiling. Orange mist spilled into the room. "Good grief," said the Doctor, trying frantically to fathom out the controls set into a wall panel. Each android jerked into life, stiffly lurching towards the Doctor and Peri.

"Now don't panic!" The Doctor tried to reassure Peri—and himself. The androids were very close. "I can't stop them! But I think I can divert them, galvanise them into one united action." Desperation drove the Doctor on. He did not know the androids were starting to rock from side to side. Then each one steadied, recovering from its drunken behaviour, and lurched over to the door. The appearance of each android was equally unstable now. The outer disguises they wore were slipping. Artificial plastic faces and wigs they wore dropped to the ground, revealing smooth metallic heads. The leading android, still bizarrely dressed in the clothes of Walpole, smashed the door from its hinges. The other androids followed it out of the cellar. As the last one stumbled out, the Doctor sighed with relief. "That's the worst costume party I've ever been to!" He began to make lightning adjustments to the black box he carried.

"Where are you sending them?" Peri asked.

"I'll have to lead them, they receive orders on a certain radio frequency. I'm adjusting this so that it transmits that frequency. They should follow me

everywhere I go. Understand?" the Doctor asked breathlessly, then ran off at breakneck speed down the secret passage, through the cellar (pushing through the disorientated androids), up the stairs and out of the inn into the street.

Peri barely had time to notice the crude mud road and wooden buildings of London in 1720. The Doctor paused, and the androids emerged from the inn, following his black box. "Excellent! It's working! We'll have to run, their actions are becoming more fluent." The Doctor and Peri led the staggering procession through the deserted streets of London, like the Pied Piper, thought Peri.

"Must be early in the morning," Peri suggested.

The Doctor grinned mischievously. "It's a good thing there's no one about—they'd have a nasty shock!"

Peri smiled in response, and looked back at the androids who followed, dressed in the fashions of the forthcoming two hundred and sixty six years.

Suddenly Peri grimaced. "What's that smell?" she said.

"Superlative! That is the smell of the black River Thames," he said grandly, adding quietly, "It's rather niffy in 1720. Not a very hygienic time." For the second time that day, Peri had to endure an awful smell.

The Doctor stood on the riverside, hand shielding his eyes. He noticed a nearby rowing boat moored to the bank and waded through the mud to reach the boat, then placed the transmitter in it and set it adrift. The swell of the dirty Thames carried it away. The undiminished attraction of the transmitter drew the androids to the Thames, and they waded in until each one disappeared under a collection of rising bubbles. The android Prime Ministers had met a watery end. The Doctor beamed. "Well, I think I handled that quite successfully!" he said.

"Really? What about the guy we're after? He could build more androids."

The Doctor agreed, but why build them?

Minutes later they arrived at the inn. Inspection soon found the time machine, in a low-roofed back room. "What a mess!" Peri commented. The machine consisted of a bewildering mass of tubes and wires dangling over, and interconnected with a bare metal frame. The centre of this tangle contained a chair.

The Doctor eagerly examined the machine. "I think it can only manage short hops, otherwise the pilot would die," he said. "It isn't in the same league as the Tardis!"

Peri had had enough of all this.

the inn."

A look of fury clouded the creature's face, but the Doctor continued. "I won't bother with it anymore, just return through the Time Wake to 1986," he suggested airily.

"How dare you? I am Tasq, Time Engineer from Bestonas!"

"Yes, insufferable big heads, so I've heard. Anyway, that machine's very unstable; energy dissipation or wastage caused the gaping Time Wake."

Peri was bursting with curiosity. "Why copy all the Prime Ministers?" she asked.

"My vessel crashed on Earth in 1986, England. I time-warped my vessel to 1720. My androids would replace all the PMs up to 1986, and under my intervention, history would change. The androids would allocate more money towards research. People such as Charles Babbage, the father of Terran computers, would benefit. By 1986, Earth could have intergalactic vessels, one of which I would steal."

Tasq's ruthless plan outraged the Doctor. "A risky—and doomed—plan. Interfering to such an extent in the history of a sentient

The Doctor had said the Time Wake would close, and if that happened they would be trapped in the eighteenth century. "Doc, come on, the Time Wake is getting smaller every second!"

Peri was right, the Doctor knew the danger, but he had to dismantle the machine. "If I remove one vital part from the machine it will be rendered useless." He paused, considering, then in a blur of speed he ripped a large silver cube from a central pedestal in the framework. "The Primary Polarity Enhancer, that should do it! Quickly, to the cellar!"

The Doctor arrived like a whirlwind in the cellar, Peri close behind. The end of the Time Wake, glowing on the cellar wall, was much smaller. "Contraction was quicker than I thought," warned the Doctor.

Peri cried, "Hurry, Doctor!" as they ran towards the white circle.

But before they could reach it, the cloaked figure barred their way. He was humanoid, with a dark blue skin of a scaly texture. His deep voice resonated through the cellar. "You destroyed my androids?"

The Doctor ignored the question. "My name is the Doctor, and this is Peri. We followed you through the Time Wake left behind by that proposterous machine in race is against the moral statutes of all travellers."

"Anyway, we've got a piece of your..." Peri began, before the Doctor could stop her.

"Give it to me!" yelled Tasq.

"Get behind me, Peri," commanded the Doctor as Tasq produced a laser pistol and levelled it at him. The Doctor brought the vital silver cube from his pocket, then Tasq watched in horror as he began to juggle it. "Now, Tasq, a deal," the Doctor confidently stated.

"No!" shouted Tasq.

The Doctor tutted sadly, throwing the cube higher from hand to hand.

"All right!" Tasq agreed hurriedly.

"Go, Peri!"

Peri realised that if she argued, she could endanger the Doctor even more. She jumped into the circle of light and, seeing her depart, the Doctor was satisfied. "You can still leave through the Time Wake, Tasq," the Doctor coaxed. "I have a time machine of my own, I could take you to your home planet."

"You lie!"

This angered the Doctor. "If that's your attitude..." he began, suddenly lunging at the white hole with incredible speed. He disappeared, landing feet first in the London sewer of 1986.

Peri's anxiety gave way to relief. "You're safe."

The Doctor smiled, smashing the cube from Tasq's machine. "Quickly, get clear!" he said in alarm. The Time Wake was collapsing, the light circle shrinking. Suddenly a blue hand emerged from the circle, like a drowning man's above quicksand. The hand was then sucked back and the Time Wake disappeared forever. "Tasq died as the vortex healed, collapsing on itself," said the Doctor wistfully.

Then his mood changed, and he bounded up the ladder, out of the sewer. The sun greeted them as they walked back to the Tardis. The Doctor sniffed the inside of his coat.

"What's the matter?" Peri asked.

"I think I need a bath."

PULL TO OPEN

INTERFACE

Peri looked in disdain at the image on the Tardis viewer. It was dark, and rain lashed the bare rocks, which were occasionally illuminated by vicious flashes of forked lightning. She turned her gaze to the Doctor, still sprawled beneath the hexagonal console, tampering with circuitry using a probe from the nearby tool kit. It caused strange fluttering electronic tones to emanate in rapid succession from one of the console's facias.

He muttered under his breath; he was no keener than she was to be on this planet. He finished his curious mumbling incantation, rising to his feet. "I don't understand it, Peri," he said, shaking his head. The Doctor had not said why they had materialised on Ketra VIII; it seemed he did not know why.

"It's awful. Cold, dark, raining," said Peri.

"Don't be negative, Peri, the air's breathable, I think." The Doctor busily regarded a number of screens set in the console. "There's a structure nearby. I'll take us there, it might be an improvement."

The time rotor briefly rose and fell, then stopped. The viewer showed dark stone walls and rain lashing down, more fervently with each gust of wind. The picture moved upwards, climbing the wall to a needle-shaped tower. The pointed stone structure was lit vividly by lightning, and a window near the top was illuminated. The weak rectangle of yellow light cast its pallid light over a small area of the grey stone surrounding it.

"We're in the courtyard of some castle, but judging by the creepers lacing the walls, it hasn't been used for some time," commented the Doctor thoughtfully.

"It's ugly," replied Peri parsimoniously.

"Of course, most castles are supposed to appeal to the attackers' tastes," the Doctor said with mock sarcasm.

"Really though, Doctor, what should we do?"

"I think it best if we find out what's up there—and why we were forced down here," he replied.

With that, the Doctor dematerialised the Tardis once again, and they arrived in a dark, narrow stone corridor in the tower. Peri shivered as she stepped out with the Doctor. They looked out of an open window nearby. The rain thrashed at the castle walls and the wind swirled eerily, howling like a tortured banshee spirit as it threaded through the castle's promontories.

At the end of the passage was a heavy wooden door. It was slightly ajar, allowing a strip of yellow light to pierce the passage's gloom. Peri and the Doctor crept noiselessly up to the door, and the Doctor peered furtively through the gap. He pushed the door open, and it gave surprisingly easily, with a creak of unoiled hinges.

Within was a flickering real fire, logs crackling, burning in yellow and red flames. A long rough table, two armchairs and a few oil lamps were the other noticeable features of the round, stone-walled room. The Doctor examined the fire; no heat came from it. He passed his hand through it, to Peri's alarm. "An illusion, Peri, a three-dimensional picture. Someone has gone to a lot of trouble to bring us here."

Peri picked up a scroll of paper lying on the table, tied with an orange ribbon. "Doctor," she called.

He came over and examined the scroll. "Ribbon of the High Council of Time Lords. Typical! I was expecting some alien entity, and it's my own people who brought me here!"

"What does it say?"

The Doctor removed the ribbon and read the symbols on the page, which were totally incomprehensible to Peri. "It seems the High Council *did* direct us here. No wonder I couldn't find the fault. We are at the centre of a time convergence, a 'bottleneck' if you will, in the space/time vortex, where time streams are

constricted, brought together so closely that they could meet, with disastrous consequences."

"Who's responsible?"

"No one, it's a natural phenomena that occurs extremely rarely. Unfortunately," added the Doctor, raising his voice so that someone not present could hear, "the Lord President lured us here to deal with it."

"What do we do?"

"Well, we have to find the exact centre of the time convergence, the point where the trapped time streams will meet, the Interface." The Doctor lit the candles on the three branching arms of the candlestick holder, then led the way out into the passage, past the Tardis and down a number of flights of stairs. The wind whipped through the castle, causing the little yellow flame of the Doctor's candle to flicker, sending strange dancing shadows to the periphery of its luminescence..

The stone passageway ended and opened onto a wider, wood panelled interior, and they trod upon threadbare carpet and creaking floorboards. The corridor had obviously been well used during its lifetime, for the panels were discoloured with age.

There were five doors on each side. Peri and the Doctor opened each one, and each time they were confronted by the same sight: dust and cobwebbed interiors, with long unused beds.

Peri and the Doctor descended a flight of steps at the end of the passage.

The ground floor was a wide-open space, bare of furniture.

The Doctor held the candlestick high over his head, the light spilling over the walls. The walls seemed insubstantial, shimmering in ghostly waves.

"Is this the Interface?" asked Peri.

"Could be, Peri. Quite honestly, I'm not sure what to look for!" The shimmering effect was spreading along the floor towards them. "The points where the time streams are being forced together are becoming more unstable."

The Doctor pulled at Peri's arm, leading her upstairs. They reached the corridor of bedrooms they had just left, but suddenly Peri stopped. "Doctor, listen!"

The noise, at first, seemed to be a curious ringing reverberation, but it then resolved itself into music, a haunting lament. The doors shimmered in nauseating waves.

"Stay here, Peri, I'll fetch the Tardis. This must be the point of Interface. Observe everything, it could be important," said the Doctor, and he hared off down the corridor, toward the stone passageway.

Peri was left, feeling extremely uneasy. What had he meant, 'observe everything'? What did he expect to happen?

Suddenly the bedroom doors disappeared and Peri nervously walked into the middle of the corridor. She could see into the rooms. The beds and dusty furniture had gone, replaced by an omnific whiteness. The music grew louder and, as Peri watched, one room changed into a sort of eating area. Women in long, frilled dresses fetched and carried for men at a long heavy table. The men laughed and sang along to the ethereal music being played.

Then the scene changed to one of carnage. The men were sprawled on the table and floor, huge spears fixing them, and a group of strange, tall figures stood over the bodies.

"The rivals of the family who originally lived here slaughtered them, perhaps centuries ago!" said the Doctor over her shoulder.

Peri turned to see the Tardis in the corridor.

"This is the Interface. The Tardis is rigged now to dissipate the convergence of the streams."

They watched as the scene of death disappeared, the feast scene returned, then disappeared again, leaving dusty bedrooms. The Interface had gone.

Behind the Scenes at Doctor Who

Make up

by Brenda Apsley

Make up plays a big part in a series like *Doctor Who*, and I went along to the BBC recently to talk to Dorka Nieradzik, a make up designer who has worked on many *Doctor Who* stories, to find out about her work.

When does a make up designer first become involved?

When a make up designer is first allocated to a programme, ie *Doctor Who*, she is sent a rough draft of the script from which she forms her first ideas of how she sees the characters. Within a matter of days there will be a production meeting called by the producer, John Nathan Turner, and the director who has been employed to work on that particular story. The costume designer, special effects designer and set designer will also be present at this first meeting.

The characters will be thoroughly discussed by everyone present. The next stage is to meet the actors cast for the appropriate part and do fittings for wigs, false teeth (if they are to be used), and face casts if necessary. It is at this point that the actors may wish to contribute a make up suggestion, eg the use of a beard or moustache. This new idea would be passed on to the producer or director for approval. It is John Nathan Turner, the producer of *Doctor Who*, who will have the final word on what is accepted or rejected.

Directors, actors, make up designers, costume designers etc, will change for each story but John Nathan Turner is the producer on all the *Doctor Who* stories. It is he who ensures that a monster make up is not a replica of a design that has been used in a previous story.

How is the 'look' arrived at?

In *The Revelation of the Daleks* there was a script note: "The mutant is humanoid in shape and is dressed in rags. His face is grotesquely distorted as though his skin has been melted. Large globs of flesh seem to have bubbled, then set before the features have had time to completely dissolve. His hands are the same"

Not only did Dorka disfigure his face and hands as in the script note, she also had special

teeth made to look as if they were in the process of melting away. She also left some hair on his head to give a pitiful look to the character and make him less frightening and more humanoid, as if Davros had been experimenting on this man and this was the result of the experiment.

A character is not always so fully described by the writer, eg Mr Jobel: "He is fat and greasy haired".

Dorka decided that, as his job was Head Embalmer, and that he would be wearing a simple blue tunic, she would make him a Mr Teasy Weasy character (an over the top old-fashioned hairdresser type). She gave him an obviously Marcel-waved auburn toupee which deliberately did not match his own grey hair, as if he was quite vain and thought by putting on the auburn toupee it made him look younger and that everyone was fooled into thinking that it was his own hair, which of course they were not!

The description of Kara read as follows: "Tall, sexy and very much in control of herself and everyone". Thus her make up had to be stunning, yet strong, and Dorka decided on browns, blacks and golds for her make up colour chart.

How does the make up design take shape? On paper?

The make up design is first sketched on paper, and discussed with the director, or sometimes the designer will make a bust of the actor in question, and then model on this to give a very clear idea of what the finished make up will look like. Then a test make up is done on the actor, to which the director is called.

"The Grand Master Orcine is tall, slim and fit. He's in his mid forties, he has an artificial leg", was another script note. Because he is a mercenary character who had found fame for his bravery and skill, Dorka decided to give him some scars on his face (the remains of some battle). She also gave him long hair tied back in a leather thong, a 'Buffalo Bill' look.

Does the make up designer always know which actor will be playing each part?

Usually, but not always, so a make up designer may have to make some modifications to her sketches before the final make up is arrived at.

What happens next?

Once the make up design has been agreed upon, the designer does a test make up. The members of the cast are called in and casts of their faces are taken, then the make up designer models the make up on the cast. Prosthetic pieces (additions like jowls, high cheek bones, heavy eyelids etc) are made up, and the actor called in to have them fitted. Of course, with natural looks, casts are not made; they are used for the more creative make up that features on series like *Doctor Who*.

What about hair?

Hair is also part of the make up designer's job. Make up designers and assistants must be able to cut men and women's hair from any period required, from a Roman cut to a 1920s style. They must know how the different styles of hair cuts differ from other times in history, bearing in mind that the instruments used in the Roman era would give a different result to the sharp steel scissors and blades of today. Where possible make up designers will try and use as authentic instruments as possible.

For wigs and facial hair the BBC has its own

Postiche department where hair is knotted for wigs, beards and moustaches etc. A number of outside wig makers are also used. Most make up designers do know how to knot hair themselves so that if you go out on location far away from your wig makers and the hair front of the wig is not correct the designer can knot the correct hair front to the wig.

The make up designers and assistants have to be able to dress wigs as well as the artists' own hair. She has to have a good eye for shape and balance, as many times she will have to dress a wig on a wig block without the artist who will wear it being there.

How long does an average make up take?

There is no average make up time. The time will depend on:

(a) The artist's skin type.
(b) What period in time it is, eg is it a make up or no make up period?
(c) Is the artist to look younger or older? How much older?
(d) Is the artist to look like herself, someone else, or perhaps a monster?

What one is certain about is that the make up artist must be physically strong. It may take her as long as five hours to do a monster make up. She will be stooping over for that whole five hours doing her make up.

It is very difficult being a make up designer; the work is very challenging. If an artist does not feel like painting a canvas he can go away and come back when he feels inspired, but a make up artist is not able to choose what day or time she will be creative. It is something that she will have to train herself to be able to do. She paints on a live canvas (actor) who may be feeling rather nervous and giving off toxins in the skin which cause the make up to go on in patches. The designer has to know how to handle the situation without panic.

What about make up for people appearing on news programmes etc?

Make up for non-actors can be very simple. Some people look good when viewed through a camera lens – the camera 'loves them' – whilst others may not look as good as they do in real life. Women who do not normally wear any make up will not be given a heavy make up – they would not be themselves on screen, and would probably feel very awkward. The designer or make up assistant will always consult the person who is being made up, and will apply as much or as little make up as is requested. Some people flush under hot TV lights, so a little corrective green make up may be all that is needed. Actors are different, of course, as make up is part of their job, and something they are familiar with. They will often request help from the make up people, particularly at auditions when to look just right could land them a part.

What sort of make up is used for TV? The sort we buy in the shops?

For news and current affairs programmes, much of the make up used is readily available in the shops. For historically based programmes, authentic make up will be used where possible, but not where it might be harmful, ie lead-based. Grease paints are used for a more theatrical make up look, but the technique is more refined than that used in the theatre, as the camera closes in on faces whereas the audience in a theatre views from a distance. Each make up designer and assistant has a large kit of make up which they carry everywhere, and there is also a stock room at the BBC which carries special colours that may not be used very often, as well as the standard stock.

What about eyes? Is the make up designer responsible for colour changes etc?

Yes. Appearance can be changed dramatically by changing eye colour, and this is easily done with contact lenses. Teeth too can alter an actor's face radically. If a prosthetic set of very large teeth is made up to be worn over an actor's own teeth, he will be given them well in advance of filming, so that he can practise speaking naturally whilst wearing them. Dental prosthetics are designed by the make up designer, and made up by specialist dental technicians.

What qualifications and training does a make up designer have to have?

Most BBC make up designers have an art school or hairdressing background. Dorka, for instance, did both, then went on to work in the theatre before joining the BBC. Theatre experience is very useful, not only for the make up expertise gained, but also in being used to working with actors and knowing how to handle them. The make up artist is often the last person an actor will speak to before going in front of the cameras, so the make up should be a soothing experience, allowing him to think about the role. The job is not as glamorous as it sounds, and make up designers don't like to be thought of as powder puff girls – their job is mentally and physically demanding, they must be unflappable and able to think 'on their feet'. Any panic they might feel must not be conveyed to the actor! They must also be committed to the job, for it will sometimes involve quite long periods away from home. Dorka, for example, spent some months in South America when she worked on *The Voyage of Charles Darwin*.

Candidates for training should be at least 20½ years old (men and women are equally eligible) and should have a good educational background, preferably to A-level standard. They must be able to demonstrate that they are artistic and have a pleasant personality as well as the ability to deal tactfully and sympathetically with all types of people. They must have normal colour vision and will be required to undertake a practical make up test at the formal interview.

Training for make up assistants usually starts with a few days at Television Centre, during which time they will be scheduled to work alongside the more senior members of the department. This should give the trainees a realistic picture of the stamina and flexible social life which the job necessitates. They will also get to know the geography of the building and see how a studio operates. They will become accustomed to routine studio duties, such as the setting-up, stocking and cleaning of make up equipment. The next three months will consist of intensive training in make up and hairdressing techniques at the make up school, under the supervision of the Senior Make Up Designer, Training. Trainees will spend the following 20 months working, in a junior capacity, at Television Centre, their progress being monitored throughout this phase. If they attain the required standard in their work they will become established Make Up Assistants at the end of this two-year period. If they do not attain this standard, trainee assistants cannot expect to continue to be employed by the Corporation.

More information about the job?

Make up designers and assistants are involved in the production of televised material, both on film, in the studios and all over the British Isles. They ensure that facial tones and contours as well as hairstyles are in order for the television and film cameras. They also create character make up and hairstyles in whatever style or period the production requires.

On a series like *Doctor Who* there is plenty of scope for the make up designer to use great imagination, as the action often takes place on strange planets and times, but in a drama such as one which Dorka worked on, *By The Sword Divided*, the period must be thoroughly researched for fashion of the Cavalier upper classes and the working classes, and the change of hair fashion of the Parliamentarians and Puritans. She found that many people suffered from bad skin, rotten teeth and did not wash very often, but because there was a romantic element in the stories it was important to show the leading actors in the best light possible, but be more authentic with the kitchen staff and peasant workers. The style of hair was historically accurate and was taken from famous portraits of the period by Van Dyke.

Art galleries are good sources of reference for make up, hair and costume. Portraits of the time give good detail of fashion, for instead of the great individuality we have today, historical fashion was worn by all the people at court. Books are useful too, as are costume collections.

The look of people dying of fever, eg Black Death, the formation of wounds and missing limbs etc, may all have to be re-created by the make up designer. For this reason medical and forensic advice is invaluable, as are film photographs and, of course, television. It is worth pointing out at this stage that programmes are not only made in the comparative comfort of a television studio, but also out of doors, day or night, in all weathers, and at all times of the year. Whether they are doing fairly routine tasks on making up stars, make up staff are the last people to come into contact with the artist before he or she goes in front of the cameras, therefore tact and diplomacy are vital qualities. Also, programme commitments can change at very short notice and this can cause problems for people who like a regular home or social life.

Beauty and the Beast

"Well, you certainly know some beautiful places to go on vacation," said Peri admiringly, as they walked slowly by the lakeside. In the light shed by the twin suns, the water glimmered pinkly and reflections danced on their faces. Far away in the distance, hills rose blue and purple, peaked with snow, while to the east, the citadel looked like a perfect white rose, so beautifully was it carved from marble and alabaster.

The Doctor smiled smugly. "You have to admit that sometimes the Tardis and I know exactly where we're going."

Peri looked closely at him. "Yes, this time you've got it right."

"I shan't argue with you," said the Doctor serenely. "This is such a lovely place. Look, here's our friend."

Peri turned. It gave her enormous pleasure to look at the inhabitants of the planet. They were beautiful almost beyond belief. Their faces were delicate and glacial, aristocratic and noble, their hair pure silver and shining like a waterfall, their eyes the colour of emeralds. They wore flowing garments that shimmered in a million colours and swirled about their slender forms.

"I hope you are enjoying your walk," said this apparition. He smiled, and his face reminded Peri of images of angels in old stained glass windows. "I'm afraid it is a little quiet here. There is more life in the citadel."

"But it's so beautiful here," said Peri, looking around her. "I don't think I've ever seen anywhere so lovely."

"It is," replied the angel. "But we from the citadel don't spend very much of our time out here. I have heard there are savages in the hills, who descend from time to time and try to cause trouble."

"Savages?" said the Doctor in surprise. "What sort of savages?"

"I don't know. When I was younger we heard tales about the savages, how they would try to storm the citadel, or steal the youngsters. I've never seen one of them, though, and the stories seem to have died down. Still, we prefer to remain safely inside."

Peri glanced round her and shivered. "It seems such a shame. Just when I was thinking that this place was perfect."

"But the citadel is perfect. There we have no unhappiness, no hunger, no ignorance. Come inside. Our king and queen wish to meet you. His Majesty apologises for the time he has had to spend in consultation with his ministers, but now he will receive you."

"The king!" whispered Peri as they entered the citadel once again and walked through the alabaster streets, with their lush green

hanging plants and rippling streams. "I can't help wondering what he must be like, the leader of such beautiful people!"

The Doctor smiled. "Probably just as beautiful as they are," he said. "Just remember, Peri, that just because you've got a beautiful face, it doesn't mean you have a beauti ul mind to go with it. As the old earth saying goes, handsome is as handsome does."

Peri scowled at him. "Sometimes, Doctor, I think you are as bad as my old grandmother. She always used to be quoting proverbs and sayings at me. Why do they always drag everything down?"

"Drag everything down?"

"Well, make everything seem ordinary, humdrum, not quite as good as it seemed before?"

"Your guess is as good as mine," said the Doctor. "But I would imagine that it's because they all have some degree of truth in them."

"Not as far as this place goes," said Peri firmly. "I fail to see how a people who have produced so much beauty could be anything less than perfect."

"You," said the Doctor severely, "are a romantic. But I will agree that everything seems to be very nice."

"Nice!" echoed Peri in disgust.

The presence chamber of the citadel was hung with drapery of a shimmering blue-green. The twin thrones rose from the centre of that glowing colour in pinnacles of silvery icicles, and on them were seated two of the most beautiful people that Peri had ever seen. The king and queen wore flowing garments that reminded her of the colour of opals, and on their shining heads they wore crowns set with diamonds, pearls and emeralds. As she and the Doctor moved forward, the king rose and came down the steps of his throne to greet them.

"It is a great pleasure," he said graciously, "for us to be your hosts, Doctor. We hope that you and your charming companion will enjoy your stay in our citadel."

The Doctor bowed. "I know we will, Your Majesty. Peri is overcome at the beauty of your home. Our guide was telling us of the danger of savages outside the walls of the citadel. Has there been trouble lately?"

The king frowned slightly. "He should not have mentioned that, we want nothing to spoil your enjoyment of our home. But, yes, it is true that there are such people living near the hills, who think it sport to frighten our people and threaten us. However, we are safe enough inside the citadel. Now, I

would like you to see the rest of our city. My queen will show you round. There is much to see, my dear," he said, turning to Peri, "and I hope you will not be too overcome by everything."

Peri smiled. "I'll try not to be, Your Majesty, but I'll find it dif icult."

Of the tour that followed, Peri had only a blurred impression of delicate white buildings, lofty-ceilinged rooms, the lush greenery of plants, and the gentle tinkling of waterfalls and streams running through the streets.

The Doctor looked around with obvious interest, and asked the queen many questions about the construction of the citadel. Strangely, she seemed reluctant to reply; her answers were evasive and generalised, as though, the Doctor thought, she and her people had something to hide. But what could it be? His mind tackled the problem for the rest of the walk, even while he commented and praised and admired.

"And this," said the queen at last, as they stopped in front of a great white tower, "is where the king's ministers meet to discuss affairs of state. We are very proud of this tower. From its top you can see for miles around the citadel."

"Even as far as the hills in the west?" asked the Doctor carelessly.

The queen shot him a quick look. "Yes, even that far," she said. "Although there is very little to see there."

The Doctor nodded as if satisfied, but he was puzzled. Why should the existence of the savages, if such they were, be denied, glossed over? These people seemed to be behaving, almost, as though they were to

them, they might well, so we'll have to be careful."

The underground passages were dank and dark. Water dripped from the roofs to form sinister pools on the floor, while anonymous creatures scuttled away at their approach. Peri, clutching at the Doctor's sleeve, shivered and shuddered as they walked slowly along, having to stoop to avoid hitting their heads on the roof.

"I hope you know where we're going," said Peri nervously. Her voice echoed eerily.

"Well, we have to meet one of them sooner or later if we keep walking," said the Doctor reasonably. "There must be hundreds of them down here."

There were. Suddenly, as they rounded a bend in the passageway, the roof yawned upwards, and an enormous room opened out in front of them. It was more a cave than a room, in fact, as dim and damp as the passageways.

blame for their enemies.

As they turned to leave the tower, Peri caught sight of something looking at her from behind one of the smooth alabaster walls, something with tangled black hair falling forward over a hideous, twisted face and fierce black eyes. She gave a cry, and the creature drew back hastily, but not before the Doctor had caught sight of it.

"What was that?" demanded Peri. "It looked—horrible."

The queen smiled. "There's nothing to worry about. It was only one of the drones."

"Drones?"

"Our servants. They do all the hard work that we have not the time to do. That one must have been sent on an errand by his master or mistress. They should not really be on the streets of the citadel. They have their own pathways, under the ground."

There was a small pause. "Do you mean, Your Majesty, that these drones are slaves?"

The queen laughed. "Of course. They are born to it, and it helps us to perform our duties in the citadel. The drones know no other life, so they are perfectly happy. Now, you must be hungry. Shall we return to the king?"

The Doctor nodded. "That would be lovely."

"Slaves!" said Peri, later, when they were alone. "I just can't believe it! Did you see that creature, Doctor? It was hideous. And it looked at me as though it were trying to tell me something."

"Perhaps it was," agreed the Doctor. "Listen, Peri, I think we should try to find one of these drones and talk to him or her. What do you say?"

"Fine," said Peri doubtfully.

"Scared?"

"Well, a little. That creature looked so ugly. You don't think they'll attack us, do you?"

"If your idea is correct," said the Doctor, "that they want to talk to us, I would imagine that the last thing they'll do is attack us. Unless, of course, our answers don't please

In the centre of the cave was a huge fire, built of oddments of wood and branches, but which failed to give out heat. Huddled round it were hundreds of creatures like the one that Peri had seen earlier. Their bodies were twisted and gnarled, their black hair hung in tangled masses over their faces; their whole attitude seemed to convey misery and exhaustion.

The Doctor and Peri stopped dead on seeing them. They were such a great contrast to what had been seen above ground in the pure white lines of the citadel. Here there was no beauty, no happiness, no serenity except that created by extreme unhappiness.

Then one of them caught sight of the visitors. He sprang to his feet, staring at them with his hideous face.

"Doctor! You came!"

The Doctor nodded. "Yes, we came. We saw one of your number today while the queen was showing us the citadel, and Peri here thought that you wanted to talk to us."

"Come, come and sit by the fire, where it is warmer!"

The creature led them to the fire, and those near it moved back to give them room. Peri thought she had never been in such a terrible place. Ugly faces ringed her, their black eyes gleaming in the firelight. She wanted to cling to the safety of the Doctor's sleeve once again, but on consideration thought that this might be just the sort of action to provoke an attack. So she sat quietly, trembling inside.

"I'm afraid we can offer you no refreshment," said the creature sadly. "We have eaten our rations, and there is never enough to feed us all, let alone visitors. But perhaps you have eaten?"

The Doctor nodded. "Yes, we have. Now, what was it you wanted to talk to us about?"

There was a pause. The drones looked at one another, as if unsure of whether to go on. Then one of them turned his head back to the Doctor.

"Revolution," he said flatly. "They have made us miserable for too long."

"Well, I can see that you're not happy," said Peri. "I can't think of anyone who would be content with this sort of life. But I thought you were born to this? At least, the queen said so..."

"The queen!" The drone spat. "I will tell you why we have to rise up against them. We are not born to slavery any more than they are. Do you know that, many years ago, everyone was free? Everyone had the same chance to make something of themselves. Then one person had the idea of splitting the people down the centre. There is a test that everyone must take at the age of ten. Those who pass it can live in the citadel, while those who fail it must become drones and live in this squalor. We all have the same beginnings, but after they go up to the citadel, they forget us, or treat us like animals. At the same time that this test was devised, one of our scientists came up with a way of creating a beautiful people.

I don't know exactly what is done, but that is why all the people above the ground look the same—the silver hair, the green eyes. Visitors do not realise that underneath that beautiful exterior they are as hard and cruel and vicious as we look."

"But they seem so happy," reasoned Peri. "They have created such a beautiful place in which to live. They love beauty."

The drone shook his shaggy head. "They did not create the citadel. My father designed it. He was one of those who failed the test and became a drone. But he became brilliant later on in his teens. He could design beautiful things, lovely buildings, but they would not allow him to live in the citadel. The test had decided that he would be a drone, and drones are not expected to do anything but hard, grindingly hard, work. His designs were taken from him and used to make the citadel, and he was punished for being presumptuous enough to think that he would ever be anything but a drone."

Peri listened in horror.

"Surely you can reason with their king," said the Doctor. "He seemed a fair man to me."

The drones shook their heads. "We cannot talk to any of them, but least of all to the king. He has had laws passed forbidding us to show our faces above ground, except when we are especially summoned. We may not speak to one of them unless they choose to address us. Oh, there are hundreds of rules we must abide by! And if we break one of these rules, which is often, for we cannot find out what they are until we have broken one, we are deprived of our rations for two days. People down here are constantly ill, exhausted, desperately unhappy. This is why we must rebel."

"And what do you want me to do?" asked the Doctor gravely. "Before you ask for my help, I must tell you that I can do nothing to help or hinder you. The Time Lords have forbidden any direct interference in the development of any planet, and I must obey them."

The drone nodded. "Yes, I realise that. We know more than they think we do. What I wanted to do was to warn you to leave here before it starts. We are not a violent people, we do not wish to harm anyone. But those who live above the ground have fierce weapons which they will certainly use on us, and we would not like you or any other innocent bystanders to be caught in the crossfire."

"And what will you do with those who live in the citadel, should you be victorious?"

"Why, we'll go back to how we used to be—one group of people living together. We don't want to kill anyone, Doctor, believe me. But we cannot go on like this. And we *will* be victorious. I daresay you have heard of the so-called savages, who give the king so much trouble? Well, they are not savages at all, but slaves like us who have fled the citadel and now live near the hills. It is our plan to bring our revolution into effect while those above ground are fighting off an attack at the gates. After that, we will all be happy once again. We will not have a king to make harsh laws. Before the coming of the test, we were free from kings and suchlike—we will be so again."

"Do you know," said Peri, as she and the Doctor talked later, "I don't think I would want to stay here any longer, even if there wasn't going to be a revolution."

"Why not?"

"Well, having heard what happened when they devised the test to decide who was to be a drone, I can't look at one of those beautiful people without thinking how ugly their minds must be. Can you imagine it? Calmly sitting in all that beauty and splendour while there is so much misery and grief so close to them?"

"Peri," the Doctor said, "I have seen it too many times, in one form or another, to be very surprised."

RETRIBUTION

In the console room, the Doctor and Peri watched the Time Rotor cease its steady rise and fall. The Doctor flashed a satisfied smile at Peri. "Arrival, Peri! At the right place," he added confidently, "and the right time!" Proudly, the Doctor gave the console an affectionate pat. "Spot on, old girl." The Doctor continued talking as Peri operated the scanner. "We'll just be in time for Edward VII's coronation, as you asked to see it," Peri said. "Doesn't look like Westminster Abbey to me!"

The scanner showed rolling green hills, separated by long winding hedgerows. The Doctor decided investigation was necessary, and opened the doors. "I'm sure we're near London, we can probably catch a train," he added over his shoulder as he strode out, "Steam, you know?"

The weather was a pleasant surprise for Peri, brilliantly sunny. However, when they finally reached a road, the clouds were gathering. The darkened sky released heavy raindrops, and as they took shelter beneath a roadside tree, Peri said, "Well, at least it proves we're in England!"

Then suddenly a horse drawn carriage appeared on the road, its driver wrapped up well against the weather, in thick coat and scarf. The carriage passed them, then abruptly stopped. Through the open carriage window, a hand beckoned to them. The two travellers risked a soaking by running to the carriage's open door.

The carriage had one passenger, an elderly man with short grey hair and round wire glasses. His rather emaciated face expressed his curiosity at the Doctor's clothes.

"How do you do. This is Peri, and I'm the Doctor."

"Oh, my name is Robert Lawton," the man replied.

As they passed through an impressive pair of open gates, Peri said with gratitude, "Thanks for the lift. We were nearly drenched!"

"That's all right, my dear. I say, aren't you American?"

Peri smiled, nodding.

Lawton winked. "Thought I recognised the accent!"

They came to a halt before a rather austere house. "Yours?" the Doctor asked.

"Oh no, Doctor!" chuckled Lawton as they stepped out and up to the front door of the house. "This is Professor Watkins' home. He lives alone with his daughter, Emily."

Just then the front door opened and a man in a white coat appeared. He was tall and slim, with long, brushed-back grey hair, and prominent features. He pushed past the Doctor and Lawton, but he was not dressed for the weather. A young girl appeared at the front door, holding a coat. "Father!" she cried as the Professor climbed into the coach. Peri noticed she was roughly her age. "You'll catch your death in this rain!"

Watkins ignored her, removing a wrapping of blankets from the object on the carriage top. To the Doctor and Peri's surprise, it was a silver casket. "Give me a hand!" cried the Professor.

The Doctor, Lawton and the groom helped the Professor to get the coffin-shaped box to a laboratory in a back room of the house. The casket was laid horizontally on the wooden bench which dominated the laboratory. On smaller tables around it were scattered pieces of drilling equipment, ready for use.

After a quick examination of the casket, Watkins finally noticed the Doctor and Peri. "Have we met?" he asked. Lawton explained who they were and why they were there, and Watkins said curtly, "I see. Do excuse my manners. This is my assistant, Lawton, whom you have met, and I am Professor Watkins."

The Doctor was inspecting the casket. "Such precision! Where was it found?" he asked.

"A kindred spirit, Doctor? This casket was found on Middle-Hill. Apparently it landed!"

"I take it that the purpose of all these drilling devices is to break into this artifact? Have you considered it may have a passenger, an interplanetary one?"

Watkins laughed heartily. "Come, Doctor, a spaceman?" he said scornfully. "In the confines of this casket he would go mad!"

"He may be sleeping," commented the Doctor.

Seeing he was serious, Watkins' mood changed to one of grim determination. "Nonsense, I shall open this casket!"

The Doctor and Peri watched the Professor and his assistant for

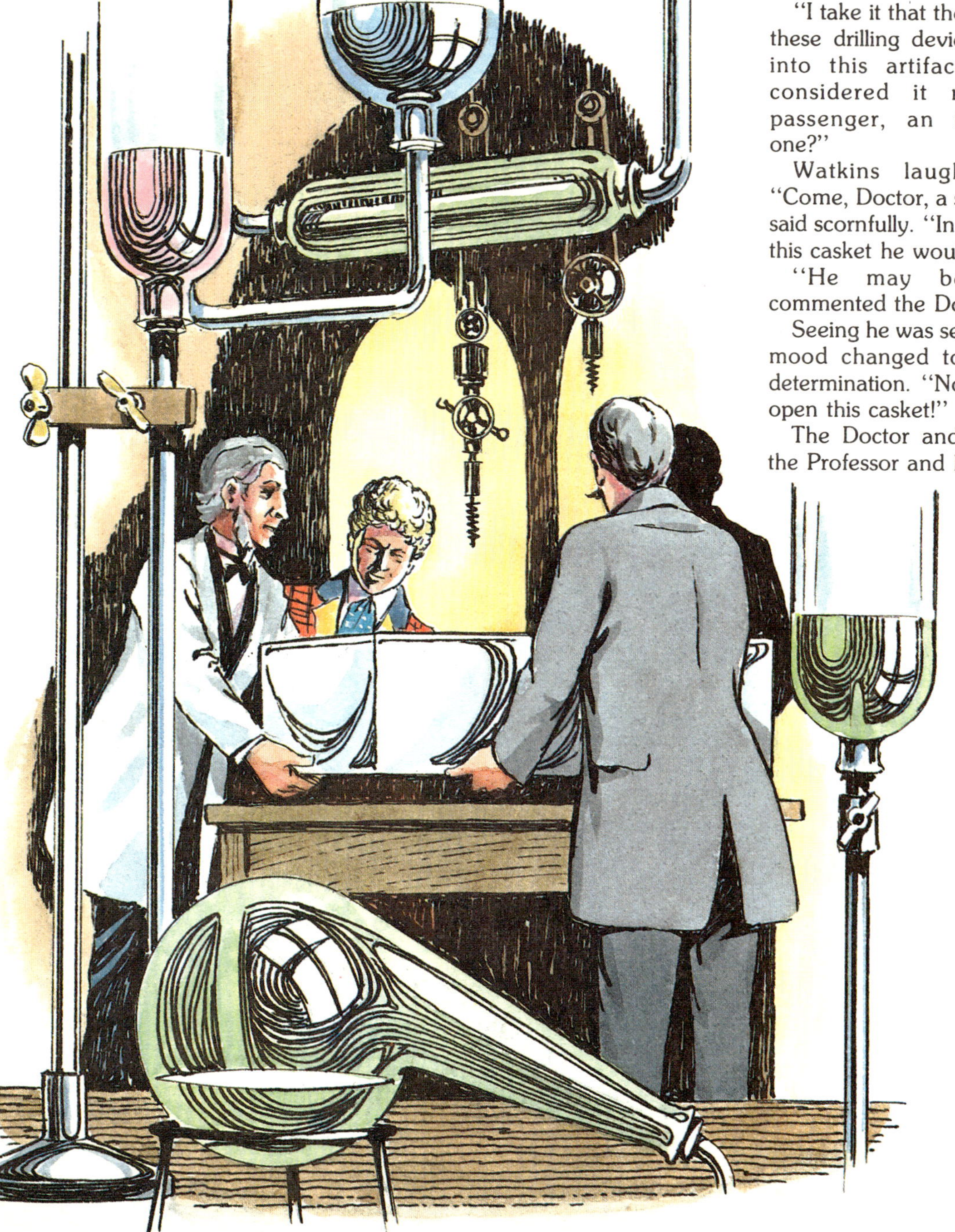

three hours as they tried to open the casket, but their drills barely scratched it.

Emily entered the laboratory. "Would you care for a cup of tea?" she asked Peri and the Doctor. They gladly accepted, and were joined by the two disgruntled drillers in the drawing room.

In the empty laboratory a cloud of vapour escaped from the hairline seal around the casket, and the drawing room was rocked by what sounded like an explosion. The Doctor and his friends ran to the laboratory. The cause of the noise was obvious. The lid of the casket had blown off; it had struck the ceiling and now lay upon the floor among fallen plaster.

The casket was empty. "It seems our guest left in a hurry!" The Doctor indicated the open backdoor.

"Lawton, fetch your shotgun," commanded Watkins. "Hurry, man!"

The Doctor walked through the open door into the garden, with its green lawns and woods beyond. It was growing dark. He knew he had little time to find the alien. Down on one knee, he could clearly see the impressions of heavy footsteps on the grass. He followed the trail, hands thrust in pockets, seemingly unperturbed at the prospect of meeting the alien.

Lawton, shotgun in hand, walked next to the Doctor.

In the laboratory, Emily and her father argued about the casket's contents, while Peri looked into it. Inside she found a box-shaped compartment with a light flashing on it.

The sun had gone down, and the alien's trail had disappeared. Forced to return, the Doctor and Lawton walked back to the house, unaware that they were being watched from the woods.

Peri showed the Doctor her discovery. "An automatic transmitting device, activated when the lid of the casket is opened. It informs the 'mothership' that the occupant of this vessel has broken his term of suspended animation," said the Doctor.

Emily was distraught. "Father, we should warn the authorities!" she cried.

"Send your groom," suggested the Doctor. "You'd be better employed barricading yourself and the girls in the house. The fewer people going out the better. You have a gun?"

"Of course!" retorted Watkins. "Old service revolver."

"Good, I shall take Lawton with me to the Tardis, to find that mothership."

Emily said, "But what about the alien? It could kill you!"

"Probably miles away by now,"

the Doctor said impatiently, and Peri noticed him tap his lapel cat. Lawton and the Doctor left, and the Professor barred every door and window. Peri hoped it was enough.

The Doctor scurried furtively from tree to tree, then he and Lawton passed through the open front gates. Finally they reached the Tardis. The Doctor fumbled in his pockets for the key while Lawton tried to read the instructions on the police box in the dark. "Come on," hissed the Doctor.

Inside, Lawton's expression was an equal mixture of fear and awe. He gazed around, bewildered by the ultra-modern console room. His mind reeled at the concept of the interior being larger than the exterior. "This isn't possible!" he said as the Tardis dematerialised.

Without warning a terrible banging noise came from the front door of the house. Outside, a huge figure hammered at the solid oak door. Having failed to break in that way, the alien turned to the front window of the house. In the laboratory, the Professor loaded his pistol. "Did you send the groom for help?" asked Emily in a tremulous voice.

"Yes, but help won't arrive for a few hours yet."

"There!" said the Doctor. "We've found and landed in the mothership."

Lawton was grasping the concepts of space travel. "On another ship?"

"Yes, just crossing Mars' orbital path. Time to investigate, Mr Lawton!"

The corridor was dimly lit, and the Doctor's pen torch was their only guide through the alien ship. "Where are we going?" whispered Lawton.

"No need to whisper!" said the Doctor loudly.

He and Lawton walked into a huge chamber. Even in the dim lighting they could see that the cylindrical chamber was of cathedral-size proportions. "Inspiring, eh? I wonder what Brunel would say?" The Doctor could not resist a smile at his timid companion's bemusement, his Victorian mind reeling. The chamber contained tier upon tier of transparent, coffin-shaped moulds.

"These caskets, Doctor..."

"I know. They remind you of our earthly visitor's. These are surely his comrades. On a ship of this size there must be thousands of them."

"Heading towards Earth? Why?" Lawton asked in horror.

"We shall discover that in due course," the Doctor replied.

In the house on Earth, the three humans were under siege. The alien smashed through the front window. "Quickly, upstairs!" shouted Watkins, and they watched from upstairs as the alien appeared. It wore a silver spacesuit, but four pincer hands and an insecteroid bulbous head with eyes of many facets were bare. The insect creature ignored them, going instead to its open casket, walking on two legs. It held a remote control box. It pressed the button and the compartment in the casket opened. Within was a laser pistol which it took out, and it then pressed a button within the compartment.

The Doctor and Lawton had walked through many identical chambers, until finally they had found the low-roofed, cluttered bridge. The Doctor busily interfered with the circuits behind the access panel of a console that he had removed. He failed to notice the blinking light on a console nearby, activated by the alien on Earth. . . .

Later, the Doctor rose to his feet. "That should do it! I've set the ship on a boomerang course home. Hopefully they won't be able to change or rectify what I've done."

He and Lawton wasted no time returning to the Tardis, but as they reached the final chamber on the way, they realised that each casket was illuminated. "We must hurry," urged the Doctor.

"What is it, Doctor?" asked Lawton.

"They're waking up! We didn't cause it, the signal must have come from Earth, which means the alien has got back into the house!"

Lawton was distraught. "The Professor and the girls!"

They hurried on with renewed vigour, the Doctor watching the creatures stirring.

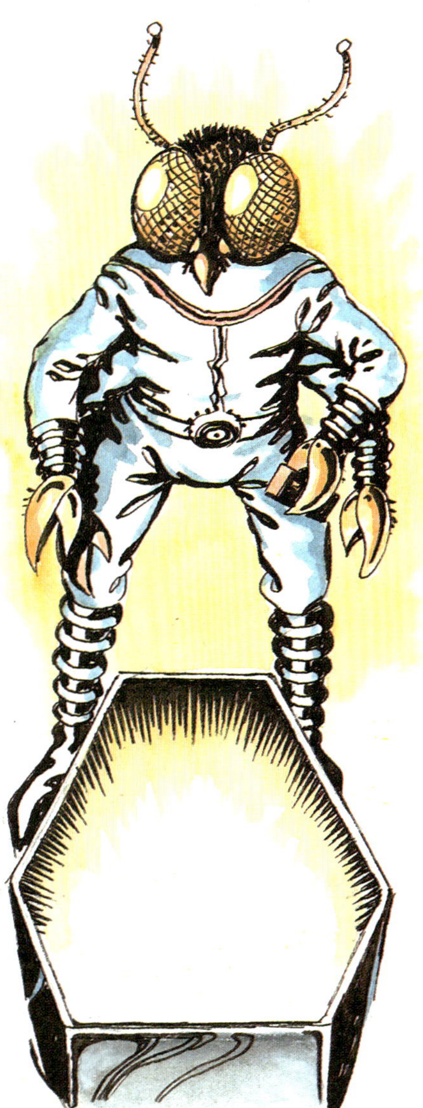

Peri and Emily were in an upstairs bedroom, and the Professor had returned to the ground floor. He watched the alien through the open lab door, then he ran forward, slamming the door shut. Without warning a laser beam lanced through the door near his head, leaving a smouldering, blackened hole in it. Recovering quickly from the sight of the weapon, the Professor ran upstairs. The anthropoid, using two limbs, effortlessly smashed down the lab door, and ran in short jerky steps after the Professor, laser in one pincer.

The Professor stood at the top of the stairs, and released a clip of bullets, but they bounced off the insect's shell.

It fired at the Professor, and he cried out, clutching the steaming point on his arm where the laser had hit. The pain burned in his arm like a hot coal. He stumbled to the bedroom where the girls hid, then slumped into a chair as they closed and barricaded the door.

In the mothership, the aliens were increasingly aware of their surroundings.

The progress of the two humanoids was hindered by Lawton's ailing strength. He stopped for breath, and the Doctor took the heavy shotgun from him. The Doctor said urgently, "Come on! Once they see us there could be trouble!" The Doctor looked at the tiers; some of the transparent doors were opening! The insects struggled with stiff limbs to climb out. "Not far now, Mr Lawton," said the Doctor, almost dragging the elderly man by the arm.

"I'm not as young as I was," said Lawton with a nervous smile.

The entrance to the Tardis corridor was very near, but Lawton was moving slowly. Then from the chamber's top tier there was a high pitched screeching. "Intruders! Intruders in the hive! Kill! Kill!" The piercing, hysterical voice caused a wave of anger and fear to course through the insect colony, the creatures screaming warning and protest. The rejuvenated aliens focused their attention on the two humanoids, and began to fire their lasers. The air crackled and hissed....

The Doctor and Lawton had by now reached the Tardis corridor, but the insects had made their way to the ground. One alien stepped from behind the Tardis ready to shoot, and the Doctor levelled the shotgun and fired. The alien reeled backwards, allowing Lawton and the Doctor to rush into the Tardis.

Peri had just finished knotting sheets into a rope as the alien started to push against the bedroom door. Peri lowered the 'rope' out of the window, then tied it to a bed leg. The alien pushed aside the barricade as Peri started to follow Emily over the window ledge. "Come on, Father!" Emily cried from the ground.

Peri added, "Hurry!"

"Go. I'll follow in a minute."

Peri climbed down to the garden. Watkins had almost blacked out in pain, but managed to reload and fire just as the alien got into the bedroom. From the garden, the girls heard his death cry as the laser was fired. While Emily sobbed, the alien appeared at the open window, then it scurried down the wall. Peri dragged the despairing Emily off into the night, the alien giving chase at a confident, measured pace.

The Tardis had landed in the woods. Lawton sat in the Doctor's wicker chair, panting from his exertion. "You'll be safe here, I'll take the gun and ammunition," said the Doctor.

Lawton watched him reload it and said between inhalations, "But Doctor, you can't be sure of a clear shot at it in the dark."

The Doctor stepped out into the night. The gun was necessary, but he hated to use firearms.

Peri and Emily sat on a log in the woods to catch their breath. A beam sizzled over their heads, igniting a tree nearby. The Doctor appeared, pointing the gun at the alien's vague outline. He told the girls to run, and they ran off into the night.

"Put the weapon aside,

human," the alien said in the high, hysterical voice of its race.

"Stop bluffing!" retorted the Doctor sarcastically. "Your mothership is on course for home."

"You have done this?" it asked incredulously.

"Yes, I've prevented a bloodbath."

"What do you know? I have good reason to hate the inhabitants of this spiral arm."

"Why? Who are you?" asked the Doctor.

"I am scout Chintor, of the Kyle system. I and the task force were sent to destroy those in this spiral arm, because a huge vessel from this region of the galaxy crash-landed on our planet. It was carrying radioactive waste. It killed millions with its toxic fallout, ruining our once prosperous world."

"So without a specific target you seek vengeance on the innocent as well as the guilty?" said the Doctor coldly.

"It is fitting for those who may have caused the death of millions."

The Doctor was furious. "Your race has suffered terribly, but that is no justification for mass slaughter!"

"Death is justification for more death. Now, your meddling shall cease!"

The Doctor guessed Chintor's intention and, diving behind a tree, nimbly rolled on the ground bringing the shotgun up as Chintor's shot missed. The Doctor fired both barrels, and Chintor, before slumping face down, made one more wild attempt at shooting the Doctor, missing completely.

When the Doctor returned to the console room, Emily asked, "Is it dead?"

"Yes," replied the Doctor sadly. "Revenge is a worthless pursuit in life."

DAVARRK'S EXPERIMENT

The sunlight filtered through the softly swaying trees; the lawn was dark green, strong under the sun's summer face. The birds flew off in flight as the wheezing of an old Type Forty exceeded their birdsong in volume. The Doctor stepped from the Tardis, tilting his face skyward and smiling. Peri followed him. The garden was overgrown. It had obviously been left for some time; creepers climbed the high garden wall. The Doctor noted how tall the grasses and weeds were, almost totally obscuring the statues and dry fountains.

A cherub stood on one foot with a harp in hand, similar to Eros in Piccadilly. The Doctor approached the statue on its long rectangular plinth, which gave the cherub considerable height. Peri grimaced at the evil little grin on the cherub's face. "It's ugly, nothing like a baby!" The Doctor chuckled and tickled the chin of the inanimate effigy, then he and Peri made their way to a house in the grounds.

The house was unkempt, with no evidence of inhabitants. The Doctor walked up to the front door, and as he pushed against it, the door creaked. "It's like being in a horror movie," Peri whispered.

The Doctor said, "The house and grounds would seem to have been left for some considerable time."

"I wonder why it's deserted?"

"Perhaps it's haunted," the Doctor replied flippantly.

They entered the house and found the dust and cobwebbed furniture intact. "This isn't right at

all," the Doctor said. "It's as if the house were frozen in time."

The cherub stood 'looking' straight ahead, but then an ultrasonic signal sounded, containing a secret code, and its head turned slowly towards the house, making a grinding noise. The cherub sprang to the ground and ran with little strides to the house.

The Doctor was perplexed. "Have a look upstairs, Peri, and I'll look around down here."

While Peri climbed the stairs, the Doctor entered the drawing room.

Peri felt uneasy. The Doctor was right: something was wrong, something evil lurked unseen. Peri found a gleaming metal ladder which led up to the attic. The ladder was obviously out of place, not of England in 1924. Peri cautiously climbed the ladder. The hatch to the attic was open, and Peri found herself standing in a well-lit room. The hatch slammed shut behind her, and she had to stifle a scream at what she saw. . . .

The Doctor scrutinised an open book which had been left on a table: it was called *Mythological Creatures*.

The cherub stealthily reached the front door, looking from side to side for his quarry. Suddenly he whirled around in time to see new arrivals at the front gates. If he killed the two humans, they might alert the new arrivals with their

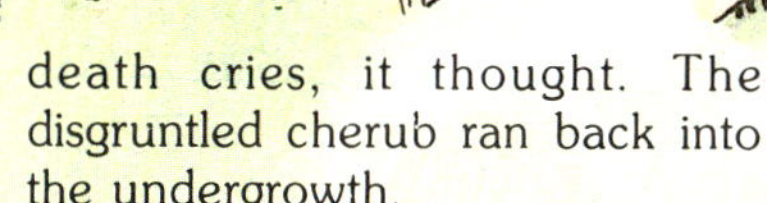

death cries, it thought. The disgruntled cherub ran back into the undergrowth.

The two workmen unlocked the gates, allowing a car with its load of two men and a woman in the Paris fashions of 1924 to enter the grounds. The Rolls Royce glided to a halt outside the house, the workmen following on foot.

The cherub snarled in frustration, showing his long yellow fangs.

The Doctor appeared at the front door as the well-groomed party disembarked. "Look!" said one man. "A tramp."

The other man said, "What's that, Charlie?" then noticed the Doctor and said with disgust, "A vagrant!"

The Doctor was speechless—almost. "How dare

you!" he retorted indignantly.

The girl with them was more conciliatory. "Charlie, Mark, please! This is a man of... breeding."

The Doctor's pride was fully recovered after her flattering remark. "I know it must seem suspicious, my turning up in your house..." the Doctor trailed off.

"Erm, yes. I'm Charlie Turner, this is Mark West, and Susan Mansfield."

"I am the Doctor. A pleasure to meet you all," said the Doctor, and he bowed courteously, much to their delight. They stepped into the house, while the workmen inspected the long neglected grounds. "Pardon me," began the Doctor politely, "but why has the house been locked up?"

"Oh, a nutter had the house for seventy years – inherited it. But he hated the house, said it was evil, so he locked it up and lived in Wales. Peculiar!" informed Charlie.

Mark added, "Then, when the old boy popped off, at the ripe old age of ninety-seven, Charlie bought it."

Susan asked, "Are you alone, Doctor?"

"No," he said, suddenly remembering his companion. "Where's Peri?"

Peri regained consciousness to find herself tied in a chair. The small attic was crammed with electronic equipment, buzzing and whirring quietly. Standing next to Peri was an upright cabinet. It was seven feet tall. Peri let her gaze wander over the instruments. How could electronics exist in 1924? She then noticed a screen on one of the consoles. It seemed to show a plan view of the house, with gardens and outlying sheds. What puzzled her were the twenty or so unmoving red dots—unmoving, that is, except for one small dot near the house. The cherub.

A creaking sound came from the cabinet, and Peri watched as a hand appeared in the widening gap. Then a horrifying creature appeared, half man, that much she could discern. But the creature had an exposed, scaled left arm terminating in a pincer. Peri could see part of his left leg, which ended in a clumsy foot, almost a hoof. Peri closed her eyes and, with great willpower, controlled her feelings of revulsion.

"Do you fear me?" he asked in a breathless, wheezing voice.

Peri looked at the creature's humanoid face. "Who are you?" she managed to stutter.

"I am Davarrk! Look at me, human, and look well, for soon you may have this appearance, or worse!" he hissed venomously.

"Peri!" the Doctor shouted as he climbed the stairs.

Davarrk listened in alarm. "Your friends are coming!"

"The Doctor," Peri said under her breath.

"Be quiet or you will die now!" warned Davarrk. He shuffled over to a screen, which showed the Doctor on the stairs. Davarrk operated some switches and chuckled coldly to himself.

In the garden, the evil cherub heard his new instructions in ultrasonic code. The afternoon sun was still bright, the sky a clear blue, and the bees buzzed around the unmoving statues. Pan's statue stood in graceful pose, blowing his pipes, as did all the classical statues. Then, just as the cherub had earlier, they began to move, legs twitching, hands flexing. They moved slowly and jerkily at first, but with growing fluency, towards the house, their grey stone legs moving at a measured pace.

The Doctor was worried by Peri's disappearance.

"Who is Peri?" Susan asked.

"My assistant," the Doctor replied, his mind elsewhere. He climbed down the stairs to a wooden door that lead to the cellar. "Perhaps she's trapped in here," he said, thinking aloud. He opened the door, and unsteadily descended the ancient, rotten stairs, into darkness. "Peri?" he called tentatively from the bottom of the stairs. He then turned on his pen torch to be confronted with a bizarre sight. On the floor were scattered pieces of broken statues, including the cherub.

"Who could have done this?" Charlie asked from the top of the stairs.

"I hope we find them," said Mark belligerently. "I'll give them a good thrashing."

"You don't understand," the Doctor said impatiently. "We're not dealing with vandals!" With that he ran upstairs out of the cellar.

In the grounds the two workmen cleared out the greenhouse as, behind them, a tall, graceful archer took aim. He fired his arrow into one man's back. The other man only had time to see his assailant before being chopped to the ground.

The Doctor looked out into the garden through the still open front door, and a statue met his gaze. For a second the Doctor was frozen in shock, then he ran forward, slamming the door shut. Charlie said angrily, "I say, are you mad? You gave me a frightful shock!"

"Look out of the window!" the Doctor nodded towards the drawing room. The three entered the room, and saw the statues striding towards the house. "Quickly!" shouted the Doctor. "Upstairs!" They all ran up to a point midway on the stairs. A fist smashed through the small opaque window in the front door, and a grey, pitted arm reached down to open the lock door. The cherub and some larger statues entered

the hall.

The three inhabitants of 1924 were bemused. "What are they?" Susan asked fearfully.

"Androids. They have the form of statues to blend in with the garden. They replaced the originals we found smashed in the cellar," the Doctor told them.

The cherub grinned mirthlessly at the Doctor, fangs protruding from its black mouth.

"Run!" cried the Doctor as he grabbed one of a pair of crossed swords on the wall. The cherub made a huge leap to reach the Doctor, who lashed at the cherub in mid-flight, knocking it rolling down the stairs. The sword blade had shattered. The Doctor joined the others on the landing, watching the cherub and fellow androids climb the stairs. The Doctor ran to a bedroom, but at that instant a statue crashed through the window, sending a cloud of glass shards into the room. The same sound of breaking glass came from all the other bedrooms. "They are very strong, jumping all the way up here from ground level," he commented wistfully. He then turned to the ladder to the attic. "Up there!" he pointed. The Doctor was last up the ladder, climbing with vigour as the androids tried to grab his feet.

He and the others found themselves face to face with the mutant. Davarrk said sarcastically, "Welcome to Davarrk's humble abode."

The Doctor walked boldly up to the still-tied Peri. "Are you alright?" he asked.

"Yes, Doctor. I'm sorry..." she began apologetically.

"Not your fault, Peri," he conceded.

Davarrk chuckled, "How touching, Doctor."

"I'm impressed by your androids," said the Doctor chattily, looking at the instrument array. "Very strong and agile. Good idea of yours to give them the form of statues. Ingenious cover."

"Thank you, Doctor, I appreciate the praise of a fellow traveller. Your method of mobility is also interesting," said Davarrk.

The Doctor was concerned; Davarrk had obviously seen his arrival in the Tardis.

"Don't bother denying it," Davarrk continued. "My androids are just as good at observing as they are at protecting me. They witnessed your arrival."

The Doctor looked Davarrk over. "A nasty case of transmorphology," he observed.

The mutant was surprised. "You know the method?"

"A little," the Doctor replied casually. "Genetic reconstitution by T.N. rays." He noticed the cabinet. "Your source?"

"Yes," confirmed Davarrk. "My vessel crashed and submerged in a nearby lake. I removed all the necessary equipment to this abandoned location."

"You experimented to change your appearance using T.N. rays. Why?"

"I wish to have a flesh and blood body to match the strength and durability of an android's. Indestructible! Infallible! Immortal!" ranted Davarrk.

"You're insane!" cried Peri.

"And vain," the Doctor rhymed.

Davarrk threatened Peri. "You, my dear, will be first into the cabinet. Do not mock me!"

The Doctor said loathingly, "I see! To achieve this 'perfect body' you need us as guinea pigs in this cabinet, so you can make the necessary adjustments."

"Correct!" said Davarrk triumphantly. "So I can find the final alignment!"

"You've failed before," the Doctor said coldly.

"My disfigurement came about by accident," Davarrk replied sadly.

Peri asked despairingly, "Why do it? It's monstrous!"

"How many?" taunted the Doctor. "How many have you

killed for your vanity?"

"Several poachers and tramps," Davarrk said defensively. "Now I have you five, I can make the necessary adjustments."

Charlie regained some of his old fire. "I won't allow it."

Davarrk's face clouded in fury. "Then you are first." He flicked a switch, and two androids climbed into the attic. Davarrk pointed a finger at Charlie, and the androids grabbed him by the arms and pushed him into the cabinet. As he screamed, the Doctor threw himself at one android, punching and kicking with all his strength. The android cast the Doctor aside as it closed the cabinet door on Charlie. Davarrk engaged the power and the machinery hummed, sending vibrations through the floor boards. Then the humming died down, and an android opened the cabinet door. The horribly mutated body of Charlie fell to the floor. Susan burst into tears, and Peri realised that she was next.

The Doctor tried to take his pulse. He gave Davarrk a fixed stare. "Mercifully, he's dead," the Doctor said. "You'll pay for that, Davarrk."

"I doubt it, for you will be next," the mutant said gloatingly.

Then a curious ringing sound came from outside. The android next to Susan was momentarily distracted by the sound, and Susan, with all her strength, pushed the android down the still-open attic hatch, then slammed it shut, pushing a bolt home to lock it. At the same time the Doctor pushed the other android into the cabinet, closing the door. The machine hummed as the Doctor and Davarrk wrestled. Susan picked up a discarded vase and smashed it on Davarrk's head. Davarrk slumped to the ground, and the jubilant Doctor kissed Susan and hurriedly untied Peri. Mark opened the cabinet and the android, joints steaming, fell to the floor next to Charlie's body.

A policeman outside rang the bell on his bicycle again, as he dismounted. He wanted to greet the house's new owner. "Hello?" he bellowed, walking up to the front door. The cherub appeared at the front door. The policeman stared in frozen terror, then with mouth still gaping open he ran in the direction he had come, with the cherub gleefully chasing him.

The bolt on the attic hatch was not enough to stop the two androids standing on the ladders, and soon their fists smashed through the hatch, splintering the wood. The Doctor scoured the banks of equipment. "The deactivation panel is our only hope of stopping them," he said worriedly.

The head of the first android appeared in the hatchway. Peri gasped in alarm. "Hurry, Doctor!"

she cried.

The policeman sprinted from the house, leaping over fallen masonry, trying to shake off the three androids pursuing him. Then an android appeared ahead of him. The policeman froze, looking back at the cherub and the other two androids as they realised he was trapped. They slowed down and started to stalk him, confident of catching their prey.

The Doctor talked to himself, frowning at the complicated machines before him while the android climbed into the attic. With arms outstretched, it started to reach for Peri's neck. "Doctor, please!" cried Susan.

Suddenly the Doctor spotted the deactivation key, and in one motion, turned and pulled it free. The android, still reaching for Peri's neck, was frozen in mid-stride. On the attic ladders, the other android was frozen as well. "I love playing statues," the Doctor quipped.

In the overgrown garden, the policeman could not believe his luck. Seconds earlier, four statues had been closing in on him, within touching distance, then they had stopped, reverting to their inanimate selves. The policeman had no desire to wait and see if they revived. With all the strength he had left, he ran from the grounds.

The Doctor stood absolutely still, eyes clenched tightly shut as Peri looked down the open hatch at the other android. "It worked!" Peri said.

The Doctor was relieved. "Of course it worked," he said, opening his eyes. The Doctor prodded the android with a finger. "Stone dead!"

Unnoticed, Davarrk had recovered, and he entered his cabinet. When it had ceased shuddering, the Doctor opened its door and the dead Davarrk fell out. But he had returned to normal, without a blemish.

Later, when those killed and those surviving had left the house, and the gates were locked again, Peri and the Doctor walked in the evening quiet of the garden. "How long will it stay like this?" she asked.

"Perhaps another hundred years," he said.

They passed the frozen figure of the cherub, and the Doctor noticed the defiant snarl etched onto its face. With a chuckle, the Doctor tickled its chin. "Now you really are a statue!" he said.

The RADIO WAVES

It began as a normal suburban morning. Washing dripped on lines in gardens, and the sounds of babies crying mingled with the whine of vacuum cleaners floated out into the street. Those who stayed at home during the day switched on their radios, listening in to the news, or to morning plays, or to popular music, while those who travelled to work also switched on as they sat, bored, in traffic jams. A very ordinary morning.

And then something happened....

On the main commuter roads, engines were switched off and car doors opened. Drivers emerged from their vehicles with dazed expressions on their faces; they never glanced at one another, but seemed to move as one person away from their cars and down the road towards the centre of the city.

In suburbia, the vacuum cleaners spluttered into silence, all sounds of children ceased. Front doors swung open, and people emerged, wearing the same blank looks as had been seen on the roads. Mothers brought their babies with them as they walked almost blindly down the streets, heading towards the city. Behind them, in their deserted homes, the radios continued to blare out into the early morning air....

"And when they all arrived in the centre of London," concluded the Chief Inspector, "they congregated outside the Houses of Parliament, and stared up at the windows as though they were searching for something... or someone."

"That's the most peculiar lobby

of Members of Parliament I've ever heard of," said the Doctor, not without humour. "Then what happened? All these people—what did they do next? Storm the building, or just go home?"

"That's the funny thing," said the Chief Inspector. "They stood there for some time—maybe an hour in all. And then—well, it was as though they all seemed to wake up... suddenly. They started looking round as though they didn't know where they were, and then they all went back to their homes and jobs as though nothing had happened. Very weird."

"As you say," agreed the Doctor.

"I wonder what caused it," said Peri. She scratched her head thoughtfully. "From what you said about the way they all moved together towards the same place, I'd have expected them to do something a bit more drastic when they got there."

The Doctor nodded. "Yes, I would think so, too. In fact, the more I think about it, the more I can't help thinking that something more drastic would have happened, but that something went wrong."

"And this only happened in London?" asked Peri.

The Chief Inspector nodded. "As far as we know. We've had no reports coming in of anything like this happening anywhere else in the country. Whatever it was, it seems to have affected only London."

"Which should please the newspapers," added the Doctor. "They won't have to go chasing off to the four corners of the country. Not that they do that anyway. Have you noticed that? Newspapers and magazines everywhere seem to concentrate almost entirely on what happens in capital cities. The rest of the country might not exist for all the notice they take of it. They dismiss all the other towns and cities as though they did not matter, and label them all with one word—the provinces. Very dismissive."

The Chief Inspector was showing signs of impatience. "Yes, well, that's as may be. You know, I've been thinking about this incident, and it seems to me as though those people were somehow led to the Houses of Parliament for some reason."

"Led?" asked Peri. "You mean there was someone with them who was inciting them to something or other?"

"No, there was no recognisable leader," said the Chief Inspector. "At least, when my lads got there they couldn't spot anyone who looked like a mob leader. That isn't to say that there wasn't one. Maybe he, or she for that matter, was too well hidden among the crowd."

"Or not actually in the crowd at all," said the Doctor.

"What do you mean?" asked the policeman. "Someone had already been in touch with them and told them to go there, at that time, and stand there for an hour looking menacing?"

"Not exactly," said the Doctor. "I don't think anyone could do that merely by telling them. People aren't stupid, you know. No, I meant some form of mass hypnotism, or hysteria, or something like that."

"Hysteria?"

The Doctor frowned. "Yes, but by that I don't mean screaming and crying. Mass hysteria means a lot of things. There have been numerous cases of it recorded in the history of many places. I remember one instance when a whole crowd of people saw an apparition that never existed. They had persuaded themselves that it was there, and so they all saw it, and would have sworn that they did. They could even describe what it looked like."

"And you think that this is what happened here?" asked the Chief Inspector.

The Doctor paused. "I don't know. I think on the whole it's more likely to be a form of hypnotism, or something similar. You see, I have come across that before, too, and this bears more resemblance to hypnotism than hysteria."

"Well, I'm glad about that," said the Chief Inspector with relief. "A hypnotist I can cope with; one man can be put away quite easily. We have slightly more trouble with hysterical crowds."

The Doctor looked at him suspiciously, but there was no sign of laughter on the Chief Inspector's face.

"So how do you think all these people were affected by whatever it is?" asked Peri. "Remember, Doctor, these people were in all sorts of places when whatever happened took place. Some of them were driving to work, and some of the others were miles away, at home. What on earth could get hold of so many people in such different places?"

The Doctor walked up and down the room for a moment. He frowned and rubbed his chin. Then he turned to Peri, smiling broadly.

"What is it," he asked, "that almost everyone has in their homes today? Something that they take so much for granted that it is almost ignored? And so much so that switching it on in the morning is almost automatic?"

Peri stared at him. "Well,

Doctor, I really..."

"The radio!" cried the Doctor. "That's the key to all this, I'm sure of it. Somehow they were influenced by a radio broadcast."

The Chief Inspector chuckled. "But, face it, Doctor, it's a little far-fetched to imagine that all those people were listening to the same programme, isn't it? How do we sort out, from a choice of over a dozen different stations, which programme it was that had this strange effect?"

"Well, of course," rejoined the Doctor, "it wouldn't have worked at all if only one station had been affected. It would have to affect all of them in the London area. And another thing—I've been thinking carefully about this, and I've come to the conclusion that this must have been a test run."

"A test run?" demanded Peri. "How do you mean?"

"Well, think about what actually happened," said the Doctor. "All those thousands of people went to the Houses of Parliament, and then after standing outside for an hour or so, they suddenly went home again as if nothing had happened. That tells me, and it should tell you too, that they were brought there for some reason. Why else would they stand as if waiting for further instructions? It seems to me that whoever is behind this was trying out his scheme to see if it would work, before he actually did what he had planned."

"But that means—"

"Quite," said the Doctor. "We don't know what he's planning, so we'll have to find him and stop it before somebody gets hurt."

"Where are we going, Doctor?" demanded Peri as they sped in a police car through the crowded London streets.

"Can't you guess?" asked the Doctor. "Where's the most likely place to go if you wanted to meddle with radio transmission?"

"One of the big radio stations, I suppose," said Peri, shrugging.

"Wrong," said the Doctor triumphantly. "You would go to

the place where all the radio transmissions have to pass."

"The Post Office Tower?" said Peri incredulously.

"Right."

"I think we'll find that the very top part of it is closed," said the Chief Inspector. "Repairs and redecoration going on, that sort of thing."

"Well, your influence should get us through that," said the Doctor.

"But how do you know that this freak is going to be up there?" asked Peri. "We'll look real idiots if we get there, after all this wailing of sirens and police escorts, and find that there's nothing there—not even a spare transistor."

The Doctor looked hard at her. "You have no faith," he said coldly. "You never believe anything I say, and you never trust me. Have you any idea what day it is today?"

"Thursday," said Peri promptly.

"It's also the eighth of November," said the Chief Inspector. "And not only that, but today is the State Opening of Parliament. That means that not only will every major politician in the country be in the Houses of Parliament, but the Queen and other royals too."

"And since Westminster was where all those people gathered for the dry run, I think we have reason to worry about their safety, don't you?" said the Doctor.

The Post Office Tower stood like a beacon in the centre of London. Lights were on in the offices on the lower floors, and very faintly as they stood at its foot, the Doctor and Peri could hear the sounds of electric drills and machinery at its top.

"I hope to goodness there's an elevator," said Peri, looking up at the great height of the building.

"Stop fussing," said the Doctor briskly. "Come on, we haven't much time."

Crowds were gathering outside both Buckingham Palace and the Houses of Parliament, looking forward to seeing their leaders dressed in splendour and finery. The Queen would soon appear, glittering with jewels and with the against him. No, I was thinking of the workmen up there. It would seem to me that they must be under some sort of hypnotism too, because they must know that there's someone up there, tampering with the radio waves. For them not to interfere, they must be in his power—and that means that they won't take kindly to unwelcome visitors like us."

"Doctor, I'm not looking forward to this," said Peri uneasily.

The Doctor grinned. "What, with these three burly policemen to protect you? Not to mention my skill in dealing with things like this? What can you possibly be frightened of?"

great crown shimmering and flashing on her head, while other members of her family followed her to Westminster, resplendent in silks, satins, diamonds and pearls.

Meanwhile, at Westminster, the Members of Parliament and the House of Lords sat waiting for her to arrive. All were dressed in their best clothes, all but a very small minority had forgotten their political differences in the excitement they felt at witnessing a ceremony such as this—and of having the people of the country seeing them at their best.

In the suburbs, those who were too busy or had no interest in the day's events, got on with their chores, and turned their radios on once more.

Quickly, the Doctor, Peri and three policemen got into one of the lifts inside the Tower. The Doctor pressed the top button, and the lift shot up.

"Have you any idea of who might be behind all this?" asked the Chief Inspector.

The Doctor nodded. "I think I may have. Of course, it might quite easily be any idiot, trying to make a point. But I think that it will turn out to be an old adversary of mine. It's right up his street. Are your men armed?"

"Yes, they are. Why? Do you think this man might be dangerous?"

"Oh, he's dangerous, certainly," said the Doctor. "But your weapons would be useless

"I could make a list, if you have a spare week," said Peri grimly.

"We're here," said the Chief Inspector, as the lift came to a stop and the doors slid open.

Out in the suburbs, people left their houses and cars. They moved slowly but deliberately down the streets, and on to the main roads into the city centre. It was like a repeat of the events of a few days before, except that this time the people carried objects in their hands: carving knives, spanners, scissors, skewers and hammers.

Meanwhile, there was a burst of activity and excitement from Westminster. The royal coach drew up outside, and the Queen stepped out. She made her way slowly into the Houses of Parliament, accompanied by ushers and bodyguards. Other members of the royal family followed her inside. Tiaras and coronets sparkled in the sun, necklaces and rings flashed, rich materials shimmered.

"Now," said the Chief Inspector, "we'd better not have any rough stuff from you, my lads."

His words seemed to make no impression on the minds of the three workmen who advanced upon their visitors, drills and pickaxes raised menacingly. The two constables with him drew their revolvers, but the Doctor signalled to them to relax. He pulled something out of his pocket, something that flashed in the sunlight as he twirled it round and round in his fingers in front of the men's eyes.

"I wouldn't bother with those things if I were you," he said calmly. "You don't want to make trouble for yourselves, do you? Now, why don't you put them down and sit quietly while we get on with our business here?"

In his fingers, the object spun and glittered, sending flashes of light spinning round the dusty, almost derelict room, and dancing on the faces of the workmen. Slowly they turned away, and moved like sleepwalkers to sit upon the floor.

"How did you do that?" hissed Peri in the Doctor's ear.

"What? Oh, it's simple," he answered, and led the way across the room to a door on the far side. "This part might not be as easy. Ready?"

The two constables threw open the door of the room. Bending over a complex array of equipment by the window was a figure that the Doctor recognised at once. He turned swiftly as they entered, and his face twisted into a smile.

"Well, Doctor, how nice to see you again."

"You!" gasped Peri. "The Master!"

"So glad to meet you again," said the Master, bowing courteously.

"I wish I could say the same," replied the Doctor. "However, I must admit I'm pleased to have found you while there is still time to stop you."

"Stop me?" The Master looked astonished. "I'm sorry, Doctor, I don't quite understand what you mean..."

"You're trying to destroy all those people!" cried Peri. "You're going to make all those people in the suburbs come into the centre of London and destroy all the politicians and the royal family!"

The Master laughed. "Really, my dear, do you think anyone

would really miss them? As far as I can see, they've done more harm than good so far to this country."

"But not half as much harm as you would do if you were to take over the place," said the Doctor. "Now, let's stop this farce, and send all those poor people back to their homes in peace."

The Master surveyed him, and his gaze travelled to the guns held by the two constables. "Since you have superior weaponry at your service, Doctor, I can see that I have little choice. You will, I think, permit me to switch off this device before we go?"

The Doctor looked steadily at him.

Outside the zombie-like crowd of people moved closer to the Houses of Parliament, while inside the House of Lords, the Queen settled her glasses more firmly on her nose and began to read her speech, oblivious to what was happening in the streets.

"Yes," said the Doctor at last, after what had seemed to Peri to be a very long pause. "Switch it off."

"Thank you, Doctor," said the Master politely. He smiled at his old adversary, turned his back, and began to flick switches and push buttons.

There was a whirring sound, which grew louder and louder until the room itself seemed to spin. Peri found that her sight began to blur, until she could see three Doctors, three Masters, three ranges of controls. The whirring sound grew louder and louder until she was almost deafened. Trying to focus through half-closed eyes, she saw the Master turn and smile maliciously at the Doctor. Then the Master seemed to grow fainter, and to waver in her sight, until finally she knew that he was disappearing. She tried to call out, to warn the Doctor, but her voice would not come, and in any case, she suddenly realised that the Doctor must have known that this was the Master's aim.

Outside in the streets, people stopped moving forward and began to look around them, bewildered, wondering where they were and what had brought them there. Inside the Houses of Parliament, MPs tried to stifle their yawns as the Queen's speech continued. Everyone knew what she was going to say anyway; everyone knew the Prime Minister's office had written the speech. It was just another humdrum State opening. Nothing new, nothing out of the ordinary....

POLICE BOX